Dreamland

NOAH KLOCEK

WALKER BOOKS
AND SUBSIDIARIES
LONDON • BOSTON • SYDNEY • AUCKLAND

Amelie loved everything about bedtime.
She loved wrapping up in her favourite blanket.
She loved listening to bedtime stories.

More than anything, she loved to dream.

But her dreams
were often hard to find.

Most nights, Amelie had to
set out in search of them.

Along the way, she was slowed by
the cold she felt in her toes …

and the uncomfortable spots in the bed.

She struggled past the moonlight that fell in her room ...

and waded through the blankets
that seemed lost in the sheets.

She marched by
the darkness in every corner ...

and tamed all the shapes

that hid in the shadows.

She danced past the tick and tock
of the clock …

and travelled beyond the whistle of a distant train.

and far

She travelled high

and wide.

She travelled low

and deep

and dark.

Until somewhere in the night,
Amelie stumbled upon slumber …

and found herself in her favourite dreams.